The Very Snowy Christmas

Diana Hendry

Jane Chapman

LITTLE TIGER PRESS
London

It was Christmas Eve.
Big Mouse was making
cheese pies. Little Mouse
was making paper chains.

"Happy Christmas to us!
Happy Christmas to us!"
sang Little Mouse. "Big
Mouse, can I decorate
the Christmas tree now?
Can I? Can I?"

For my grandson Ruairidh –
Happy Second Christmas, with love
– D H

For Jim (Big Mouse) and Raechele (Little Mouse)
– J C

LITTLE TIGER PRESS
An imprint of Magi Publications
1 The Coda Centre, 189 Munster Road, London SW6 6AW
www.littletigerpress.com

First published in Great Britain 2005
This edition published 2011

Printed in China

2 4 6 8 10 9 7 5 3 1

"We'll do it together," said Big Mouse.
Little Mouse hung golden acorns and
mistletoe berries on the tree. Big Mouse
put a star on the top.
    "But we've forgotten the holly!"cried
Little Mouse. "I'll go and get some."
And off he rushed.
    "Mind it has nice red berries!"
called Big Mouse.

Little Mouse set off down the path singing, "Jolly holly! Holly jolly! Jolly holly Christmas!"

But there was no holly to
be seen on the first corner.

And no holly on
the second corner.

And no holly on
the third corner.

Over the bridge ran
Little Mouse and at last
he found a holly bush with
shiny red berries. He jumped
up and down with excitement.

"Oh jolly holly! Holly jolly!
Jolly holly Christmas!" sang
Little Mouse, stretching high
on his toes to reach some.

But suddenly soft white flakes started falling all
round him. One flake fell on Little Mouse's nose
and made him sneeze. "Goodness me!" said
Little Mouse. "The sky is coming undone!"

Little Mouse began to hurry
home. Lots more pieces of sky
were falling on him. Faster and
faster they fell. They fell on his
ears and his whiskers and his tail.
"Oh dear, oh dear," said Little Mouse,
"I'd better take some of this to show
Big Mouse. He'll know how to stitch the sky
together again."

Little Mouse made a ball of
white flakes and put it in his bucket.
Back over the bridge he hurried.

Suddenly he saw a strange creature
in the water, making faces at him.
It had lots of ears and a squiffy face,
and it waved its arms at Little Mouse.

"Ooooh!" squeaked Little Mouse.
"It's a Mouse Ness Monster!"
and he fell on his bottom.
   "Oh, I wish Big Mouse was here!"
he cried, scrambling up.
   Back down the path ran Little Mouse,
looking over his shoulder to see if the
Mouse Ness Monster was following
him. It wasn't, but something was!
Little Mouse could see its paw prints
coming after him.

"EEEEKkk! HELP! EEEEKkk!"
squeaked Little Mouse. "Now there's
an Invisible Monster chasing me!"

Little Mouse ran up
and down and round and
round in circles to escape,
but the paw prints of the Invisible
Monster went up and down and
round and round after him.

Little Mouse ran and ran.
Faster and faster whirled
the white flakes and faster
and faster ran Little Mouse.
And still the Invisible
Monster followed him.

At last Little Mouse saw
his house. But there in the
garden was a huge White Mouse!
"Oh no, no, no!" squeaked Little
Mouse. "Another monster
waiting to catch me!"
Little Mouse trembled
and began to cry.

But then the front door
opened and there was
Big Mouse. Little
Mouse leapt into
Big Mouse's arms.

"Big Mouse, Big Mouse," he cried,
"the sky has come undone! And look!"
he wailed, pointing to the paw prints.
"An Invisible Monster has been
following me, and there was a
terrible Mouse Ness Monster in
the water, and now that scary
White Mouse is staring at me!"

"Oh, Little Mouse," said Big Mouse,
"the sky hasn't come undone.
It's SNOWING!

"And there aren't any
Invisible Monsters.
Those are your paw prints.

"And that Mouse Ness Monster
was your reflection in the water.
Look!" And Big Mouse showed
Little Mouse his face in a puddle.

"And this is a snow mouse I made to welcome you home," he said. "Let's make another." And so they did!

"Snow is magic!" cried Little Mouse.
"Yes," said Big Mouse. "Father Christmas likes snow too!"
Little Mouse jumped up and down. "Will he be here soon? Can I hang up my stocking now?"
"You can," said Big Mouse. "Let's go and get warm first."

So in they went and warmed
their paws by the fire.

Little Mouse hung up his
stocking and Big Mouse hung
up his stocking too. The holly
berries shone in the firelight.

"It's almost Christmas,"
said Little Mouse. "Jolly holly!
Holly jolly! Jolly holly Christmas!"
And he wriggled his warm toes.